DR WHITE

OTHER BOOKS IN THE
NIGHTMARE CLUB SERIES

DR WHITE

BY
ANNIE GRAVES

ILLUSTRATED BY
GLENN McELHINNEY

Little Island

Dr White
First published in 2016 by
Little Island Books
7 Kenilworth Park
Dublin 6W, Ireland

ISBN: 978-1-910411-52-0

A British Library Cataloguing in Publication record
for this book is available from the British Library

Book design by Fidelma Slattery

Typeset in Trebuchet MS by Vincent Connare and October Crow by
Chad Savage. Cover title typeface also used in interior: Remnant by
Chris Au, www.chrisau-design.co.uk

Printed in Poland by Drukarnia Skleniarz

Little Island receives financial assistance from the Arts Council/An
Chomhairle Ealaíon and from the Arts Council of Northern Ireland

To all you kids on the Write to Read project
and all young writers everywhere.
Maybe I'll let you join the Nightmare Club
if you're very nice to me.
Love, Annie

Annie Graves is twelve years old, and she has no intention of ever growing up. She is, conveniently, an orphan, and lives at an undisclosed address in the Glasnevin area of Dublin with her pet toad, Much Misunderstood, and a small black kitten, Hugh Shalby Nameless.

You needn't think she goes to school — pah! — or has anything as predictable as brothers and sisters or anything as dull as hobbies, but let's just say she keeps a large saucepan on the stove.

This is not her first book. She has written ten so far, none of which is her first.

Publisher's note: We did try to take a picture of Annie, but her face just kept fading away. We have sent our camera for investigation.

THANK YOU!

There is this GANG of children and they are claiming that they wrote this story. That is total rubbish. I am a Famous Author and they needn't think they are going to steal my fame. But, look, there are more of them than of me, so I think maybe it might be a good idea just to mention their names and say thank you to them for being really great kids and lovely to know. (But they had *absolutely nothing* to do with this book — OK? No, no, it's TRUE, I wrote it. I'm the STAR! I've got the cool name!)

So, guys:

Adam Knott
Adam Rafferty
Brooke Maher
Darren Ancuta
Dylan Dowling
Jade Murray
Jordan Dignam
Niamh Shields
Norbert Koczut
Roshan Sivam
Sean Moore O'Mara

THANKS
FOR
BEING
SO FAB!

Thank you also to the St Patrick's Drumcondra Write to Read project, especialy Eithne and Marja, and to Poetry Ireland for ... eh, for being Poetry Ireland, I think.

W ell, the Nightmare Club gang gathered the other night at my house for a Nightmare Club sleepover, and this time it was Alex's turn to tell a story.

I don't rate Alex as a storyteller. I wasn't expecting much. But then ... Well, read it for yourselves.

See what you think.

'My story is about my doctor,' said Alex.

Everyone groaned.

'You are supposed to tell a *spooky* story, Alex,' said Jeff. 'We don't need to hear about some boring doctor's appointment.'

'Yeah, but, wait till you hear,' said Alex.
'My doctor is called Dr White.'

'Oooh, *spooky*,' jeered Jeff.

'*Dead* scary,' said Betty. 'I wanna go
home. It's too *much* for me.'

2

'Yeah, but listen,' said Alex. 'This doctor is not exactly up to scratch. He was giving me all this weird medicine.'

'We all get weird medicine from the doctor,' said Tyler. 'That's not Nightmare Club material.'

'Yes,' said Alex, 'but this stuff is all greeny yellow and kind of gloopy and it tastes like rotten eggs.'

'Yuck,' said Betty — like she knew what rotten eggs tasted like.

'EEEaaaagh,' squealed Sarah, like *she* knew what rotten eggs tasted like.

'Well, that's disgusting all right,' said Mark, 'but it's not exactly spooky.'

'Thing is,' said Alex, 'he said it was to strengthen my blood. But there's nothing *wrong* with my blood, see? I'm perfectly fine.'

'So why have you been going to the doctor, then?' asked Betty.

'It's my mum,' said Alex. 'She fusses. And she *likes* the doctor.'

'Hmm,' said Jeff. '*Suspicious.*'

'So, this Dr White, he took all these blood samples. He *said* he needed to send them to the lab for testing. To see what's wrong with me.

But he was taking *way* too much blood. First he used an ordinary syringe. And then he started using a double one.

Look!'

The Nightmare Club members all stared at the puncture marks on Alex's arm. They did look a bit odd.

An there were way too many of them. Like, *dozens*.

'And there was this weird smell of blood in his office,' Alex added.

Gloopy medicine?

A *double* syringe?

Loads of blood samples?

And a weird smell of blood in the air?

Suddenly the room went very quiet.

You could hear a pin drop.

'Last week, I was in Dr White's surgery,'
Alex said. 'As usual.'

'On your *own*?' asked Sarah.

'No, my mum was with me — as usual,'
said Alex, 'but she doesn't notice
the things I notice about
Dr White. He's very
charming to adults.
But I get the
impression he
doesn't much
like kids.

Anyway this van driver comes to the door. He says he's there to pick up the blood samples but I *saw* what he took away.

Whole *bottles* of blood.

They're not going to the lab, I thought to myself.

And then I spied
the label:

Take twice a day.

Dilute before
consumption.'

'Wooooooo!' went Jeff.

'Eeeeeeek!' said Betty.

'*Vampires*,' murmured Tyler.

'Come on,' said Mark. 'That's not how vampires get their blood. It doesn't come in *bottles*, like fizzy drinks. You know that.'

'I never said anything about vampires,'
said Alex. 'But wait till you hear what
happened next …

I told my mum I needed to leave the surgery, that I'd forgotten I had to meet my friend.

My mum was so busy flirting with the doctor, she hardly even noticed me going.'

'So what did you do then?' asked Tyler. 'I suppose you followed the van?'

He smirked. He did not think Alex had followed a *van*!

'Yes I did,' said Alex. 'On my bike. But I lost it after a while in the traffic. It was just too fast for me.

But, listen … That van — it was going in the direction of the blood bank, not the lab.'

'Yeah, but you *lost* it,' said Mark.

'So end of story,' added Jeff.

'No,' said Alex. 'Not at all.

Two days later my mum was reading the paper at home and I caught sight of a headline. A very interesting headline:

Man Found Dead in Park.'

'So what's that got to do with your Dr White?' asked Mark.

'Well,' said Alex, 'let's just say he didn't die of natural causes. And he was found just across the road from the blood bank.'

'So what happened him?' Betty wanted to know.

'The paper said he died of

BLOOD LOSS,

said Alex.

'But ... get this — there were no wounds on his body. The only clue was ...'

'What?' they all screeched.

'A double syringe mark on his arm. And his body was totally drained of blood.

• •

Something weird was definitely going on.

I had to investigate that blood bank. I made sure I had everything I needed: a bulb of garlic, a torch and my phone.

When I got there I locked my bike to a pole, with a double lock, and I went in the spinning doors and spoke to the receptionist.'

'Did you use the hand sanitiser?' asked Sarah.

'There wasn't any hand sanitiser. Funny that, in a blood bank.

They aren't supposed to take blood from children in a blood bank, but the receptionist didn't seem to know that.

That's how you can tell it wasn't an ordinary blood bank. This was a blood bank that had been ... *taken over*.

And, listen, there was not a mirror in sight. Nothing shiny. Nothing that might give a reflection.'

'But why would vampires be running the blood bank?' asked Jeff. 'That's not what vampires do.'

'Maybe they were running out of people to bite,' said Sarah. 'Maybe it's a new *kind* of vampire.'

Alex continued with the story:

So the receptionist escorted me to this badly lit blood donation room, and she put me up on a kind of bed and stuck a needle in my arm without even using the cold spray or disinfectant or anything.

And guess what —

SHE USED A DOUBLE SYRINGE!

I whipped out my phone while she was doing all that.

I pretended I was just checking my texts, but I took a photo of her.

Only it wasn't a photo of her. It was a photo of her white coat.

WITH NOBODY INSIDE IT.

Now I knew for sure what I was dealing with.

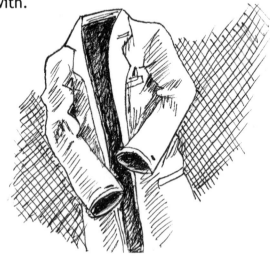

The receptionist left me lying there and then in came this other woman in a white coat.

So I took my torch out of my pocket, turned it on and shone it right in her eyes. They were a devilish shade of red.

She howled in agony at the bright light.

There was a terrible hissing noise and a
smell of smoke and all that was left of
Jennifer was her white coat and a heap
of ashes on the floor.

I knew her name was Jennifer because
her name tag fell off her coat and
clattered to the floor. Clink-clank.

Next thing, the door slammed open and in stormed another white coat. A man this time and he was *roaring*.

I had dropped my torch, but I still had the bulb of garlic.

He came right up to my bed and bared his fangs at me.

I milled the garlic right into his big gloopy gob.

And before my very eyes he melted into a gooey puddle that smelt garlicky and vile.

I yanked the needle out of my arm,
leaped up and legged it out of that room
as fast as a galloping horse.

I could see a whole bunch of white coats at the end of the corridor and they were coming straight for me.

I turned in the opposite direction and
zoomed down the corridor.

They were close behind me — I could
hear hissing, shouting and a stampede of
boots.

I ran around a corner and flung open a random door.

I went inside and closed it behind me.

It was a broom cupboard, full of buckets,
mops, brooms — and a vacuum cleaner.

I knew what I had to do. (I saw this on
Ghost Busters.)

I plugged in the vacuum cleaner, turned it on, opened the door and aimed the nozzle at the flock of oncoming white coats.

41

SLURP, SLURP, SLURP

went the
vacuum cleaner

as it sucked them up, one
by one, like a two-
year-old licking
an ice-cream.

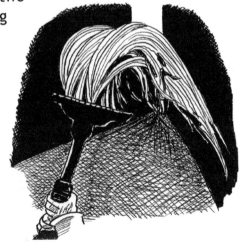

As the last one slithered into the belly of the vacuum cleaner, it gave a little burp.

But I knew there could be more of them, so I legged it out of there, out the front door and down the steps. I rushed to my bicycle, wrestled with the double lock and finally got it free.

I leapt up onto the saddle and started pedalling as if my life depended on it — because it did.

I made for the police station. I'd be safe there.

The police were kind to me. They gave me tea and biscuits.

But halfway through telling my story I felt a bit woozy and I suddenly tumbled to the floor.

THUMP

As I went out, I heard the words 'blood loss' and 'hospital'.

I woke up to the sound of a heart monitor going *beep-beep, beep-beep, beep-beep*.

I was definitely alive.

The window was open and I could hear birds chirping.

There was a vase of flowers by my bed.

It was all lovely.

A cheerful voice spoke and I realised there was a nurse beside my bed.

'You're in St Gabriel's hospital, Alex. How are you feeling?'

'I'm fine,' I said, 'except I feel a bit weak.'

'That'd be the blood loss,' said the friendly nurse. 'But don't worry, we are going to get the blood specialist to take a look at you, and you'll soon be back on track, right as rain. Ah, here he comes now. I'll leave you in his hands.'

The nurse left the room, and I turned to look at the blood specialist, the man who was going to make me better.

I looked right into his face.

IT

WAS

DR

WHITE

. . .

WWW.THENIGHTMARECLUB.COM